Three in a Balloon

Three in a Balloon

by Sarah Wilson

SCHOLASTIC INC.
New York Toronto London Auckland Sydney

ISBN 0-590-42632-X

12 11 10 9 8 7 6 5 4 3   6 7/9

Printed in the U.S.A.   08

For Herb with love

Acknowledgments
Special thanks to Marion Buckner and Ray Wagner
of the San Diego Aerospace Museum Library.

Foreword

This book is based upon the true story of
the world's first air passengers—a sheep,
a duck, and a rooster—who flew over France
in a new invention, a Montgolfier hot air
balloon, on September 19, 1783.

What would you do
if you
were a sheep
or a rooster
or duck

and your friends liked to play
in unusual ways
with balls
and bubbles
and feathers
and steam?

What would you do
if they stitched up big toys
with baskets of straw

and put you inside
on a crisp windy day

and with smoke
and hot air

sent you up in the sky?

Sent you up in the sky
over housetops
and trees,
sent you up in the sky
over farmyards
and fields

as the cows
craned their necks
and the deer
jumped away

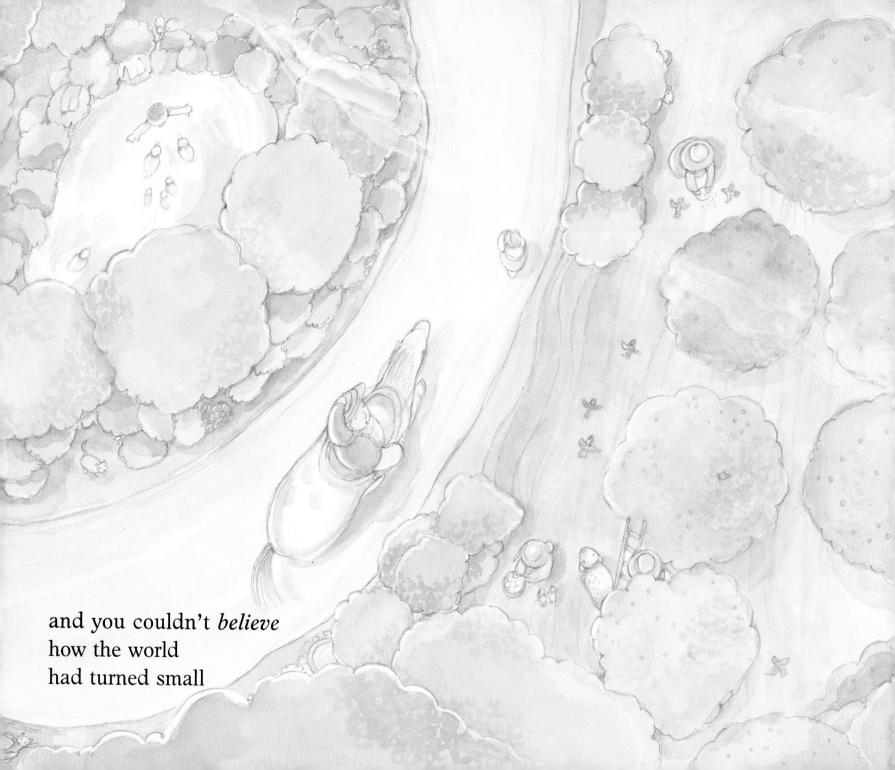

and you couldn't *believe*
how the world
had turned small

into gardens
and streams
and towns
that were toys!

And the landscape below
was as quiet as snow?

What would you do
with your feet off the ground
sailing out in a sky
turning blue
as the sea
with the brush of the wind
on your feathers
and fur?

Would you yip?
Would you yap?
Would you quack out
a cheer?

And what would you do
when little dogs leaped
for your bubble
of sun
and it slowly
came down
over forests
and hills

like a great tasseled quilt
folding into
the trees?

Would you sigh
for the sky?
Would you crow?
Would you
cry?

What would you find
in the crook of a tree
as your basket
swung free
to the safe ground
below

and you landed
like this
with a yowl
and a howl

and were cuddled
and crooned
and cradled by friends?

Would a kiss on the nose
bring you up on your
toes?

And what would you do
if they took you
to live
in the fields
of a king

and he hugged you
good-night
as the day turned to dusk
and left you to rest
on a soft bed
of down?

Would you believe
it was real?
Would you
believe
it was
true?
Would you believe
this adventure
had happened
to YOU?

Then with the wink
of the stars
overhead
and the hoot of an owl
and the coo of a dove
would you close
your eyes tight
and think
with delight
of all you had seen
on this dream
of a day
when the earth
seemed quite small
and *you* were
quite tall